D0535953

Purchased from
Multnomah County Library
Title Wave Used Bookstore
216 NE Knott St, Portland, OR
503-988-5021

I'm a

SHARK
Bob Shea

Balzer + Bray
An Imprint of HarperCollins*Publishers*

I'm a Shark
Copyright © 2011 by Bob Shea
All rights reserved. Manufactured in China.
No part of this book may be used or reproduced in any manner whatsoever without
written permission except in the case of brief quotations embodied in critical articles
and reviews. For information address HarperCollins Children's Books,
a division of HarperCollins Publishers, 10 East 53rd Street, New York, NY 10022.
www.harpercollinschildrens.com

Library of Congress Cataloging-in-Publication Data
Shea, Bob.
    I'm a shark / Bob Shea. — 1st ed.
        p.   cm.
    Summary: A boastful shark is not afraid of anything, which impresses his
underwater friends until they ask about spiders.
    ISBN 978-0-06-199846-1 (trade bdg.) — ISBN 978-0-06-199847-8 (lib. bdg.)
    [1. Fear—Fiction.   2. Sharks—Fiction.   3. Humorous stories.]   I. Title.   II. Title: I am
a shark
PZ7.S53743Im   2011   2010021850
[E]—dc22   CIP
                                                         AC

Typography by Colleen Shea, Perfectly Nice
13 14 15 16 17   SCP   10 9 8 7 6 5 4 3
❖
First Edition

This book is dedicated to Ryan
because I love him a lot.

I'm a shark!

Aren't I awesome?

(seasonal allergies)

When I get a shot, I don't even cry.

I can watch scary movies without closing my eyes.

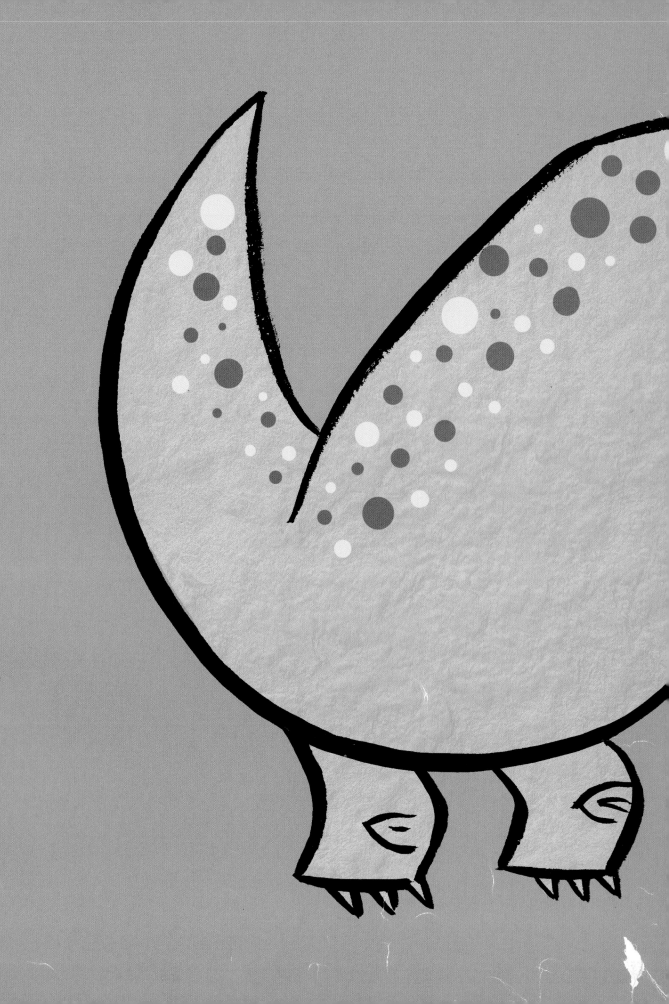

If there were a dinosaur here and he saw me,
you know what he would be?

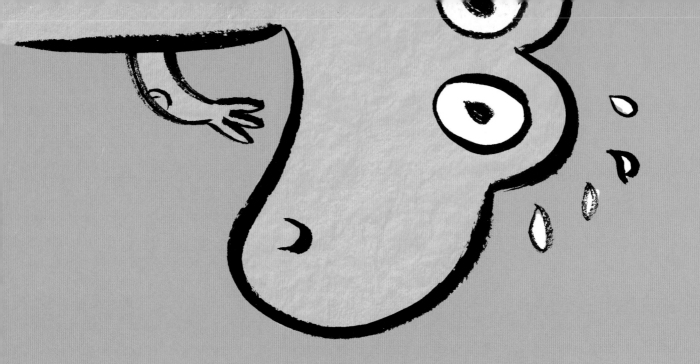

Scared.

What about a creepy spider
or a scary squid?

Creepy spider!
Yuck! Is it on me?
EWWW! EWWW! EWWW!

No, there's not really a spider.

Phew! Are you sure?
The squid isn't a spider dressed as a squid, is it?
That's how they get you!

Nope, the squid is a squid.

A scary squid that's not
really a creepy spider?
Bring him on!

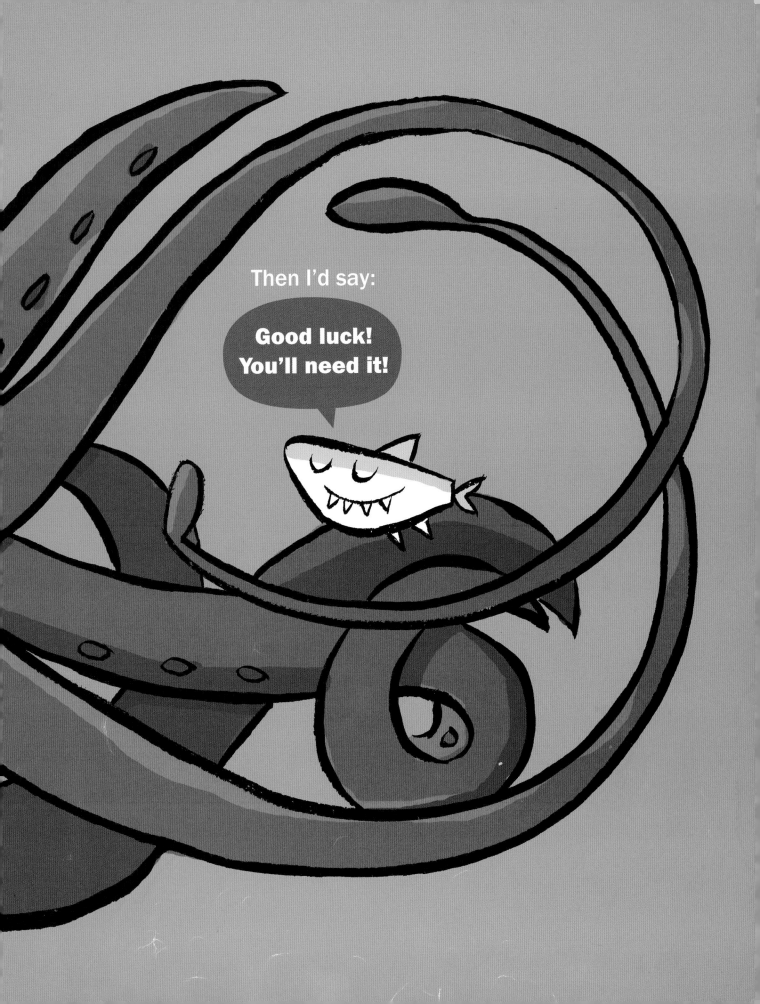

Then he'd ink himself in front of everybody.
So embarrassing!

What about the dark?
Everyone is afraid of the dark!

Is there a big creepy spider?
No.

A lot of little creepy spiders?
No, just a lot of dark.

No problem!
Close your eyes. . . .

Pretty dark, right?

OH MY GOODNESS! A TOTALLY AWESOME SHARK!

Where?

Where?

You're looking at him!
I'm not afraid of the dark—
the dark is afraid of me!
Dark heard I was coming and ran!

Okay, tough guy,
how about a big mean bear?
I bet you're afraid of
a big mean bear.

Is the big mean bear holding a creepy spider?

No.

Near a creepy spider?

No.

2 feet

**Thinking about a
creepy spider?**

No.

**Reading a book about a
creepy spider?**

No.

Nope, just you and
the big mean bear.

A BIG, MEAN,
SPIDERLESS BEAR?

Don't make me laugh!

Then I'd say:

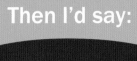

GRRRRRR?
Try rows and rows of
razor-sharp teeth!
How's that grab you,
Mr. Bear?

He won't answer—he'll be too busy
fainting, hiding, fleeing, or crying.

 Well, I guess everyone is scared of something.

I'm not.

What about spiders?

If I saw a spider, I would swim away
as fast as my fins would take me.
That's not scared—that's smart.

That's silly.